REINDEERACHE
A 21st Century Christmas

Concept, Story, Script and Production by:
BRIAN DONNELLY

Art, Pencils, Inks, Colors and Cover by:
ALFONSO PARDO

Lettering and Design by:
LETTERSQUIDS

Concept, Story, Script and Production
by Brian Donnelly

Brian Donnelly is an award-winning independent writer and publisher, a former United States Marine, a 27-year veteran of the armed forces, an elected public servant and nationally recognized attorney. This is his fourth children's book.

His first graphic novel, "Tir Na Fuil Volume 1: A Hard Rain's Gonna' Fall," won a bronze medal in the 2017 Independent Publisher Book Awards alongside fellow award winners and pop culture icons Stan Lee and William Shatner. His second graphic novel: Once and Future: Finest Hour won the Silver Medal in the 2020 Moonbeam Awards. His first children's book TOOT FAIRY, his second children's Book Help me Hide This Giraffe! and his third children's book No Bunny But Me each won a number of awards including Best Illustration and Best Cover by the Best Indie Book Awards.

Brian learned of the power of humanity in the face of suffering when He was diagnosed with a brain tumor, epilepsy and autoimmune encephalitis a few weeks after hearing the news his wife was pregnant with their daughter Brooke. He underwent 9 hours of brain surgery when his wife was five months pregnant and spent the first seven months of his daughter's life in immuno-infusion therapy. As a result, his publishing company donates proceeds from its creative works to charitable causes.

Pencils, Inks, Colors, and Cover
by Alfonso Pardo

Alfonso Pardo Martínez (aka Pardoart) was born in Madrid, Spain. He studied Fine Arts at the Complutense University, Madrid graduating in 2001. He has been attracted to artistic expression through drawing ever since he was a child, partly as a consequence of suffering from moderate dysgraphia and dyslexia. He realized that although he had problems with reading and writing, he felt comfortable and with qualities to be able to express himself with drawings. His fondness and passion for fantasy, science fiction, role-playing games and mythology helped him to improve his artistic skills by understanding that with drawing he could show what his imagination was boiling inside him.

After graduating, he began his career as an illustrator and concept artist in the video game industry in Pyro Studios doing visual development work on the video game Commandos 2. A year later he got a permanent position as motion graphic designer in the regional television of Castilla-La Mancha. Since then, he has combined this work with the realization of illustrations in different media: Film posters, book covers, editorial illustrations, board games illustrations, character development in the film, animation and videogame industry. He currently lives happily in Toledo (Spain) with his wife, his two daughters and his cat Gaspar.

"The way you spend Christmas is far more important than how much."
– Henry David Thoreau

Santa awoke with Christmas Eve dread -
Lists upon lists were filling his head.
He pulled the sheets over his head and he hid
Still coughing and sneezing from his bout with Covid.

He thought he heard shouts
And sat up in bed,
Straining to hear
What was being said.

But it was no use, he could not make it out.
So he got out of bed, ignoring his gout.
He scratched and he burped
And silently farted,
Determined to get
This holiday started.

Santa stood by his bed,
And stretched out his back.
But all he got in return
Was a **POP, CREAK and CRACK.**

When he walked down the stairs
His fears galvanized,
As Santa discovered
His elves unionized.

"SANTA!" they yelled, "You've been dodging our calls!"
"We know you've been breaking
Our Elf Labor Laws.
We all are demanding
Double time pay!
For making us work
On each Christmas Day."

"Anything else?" Santa groaned
As they yelled in frustration,
"Yes, we would like
48 weeks paid vacation!"

Santa's head was swimming from all of this grumble,
And "Anything else?" was all he could mumble.
The elves gathered 'round and started in rhyme
Listing their problems
All at the same time.

"All of us elves have too many tasks,
And some don't want to work if we have to wear masks!"

"It's all very clear in the demand that we wrote.
There's no need to be on-site, we can all work remote!"

"There are so many children, I fear we have missed some.
What we need is a computer cloud-hosted system!"

"We have the name and address of every child on Earth.
As well as their gender and their date of birth!
What we need is a written privacy policy,
And biometric online cybersecurity!"

"We need separate systems for identification,
And encrypted multi-factor authentification."

"What we need are contracts and insurance to boot,
To protect all of us from a class-action lawsuit!"

"We must start feeding the reindeer
Nothing but mint
In order to reduce
Their carbon footprint!"

"Dasher and Dancer, each don't like their name,
And Prancer just filed
A workers' comp claim."

"None of the reindeer are happy at all,
And they all are demanding
Gender-neutral sleep stalls."

"It's absolutely critical
We begin to rehearse
Delivery of gifts
In the Multiverse."

"Many letters have said
That you're nothing new,
And you don't do anything
That Amazon couldn't do."

"Despite your creation,
And delivery of gifts
Our polls show most adults
Don't believe you exist."

The older elves yelled that back in their day
Christmas was handled in a much different way.
The young elves ignored them
As all obsolete,
And resorted to complaining
By way of a Tweet.

Santa said -

"Sleep stalls and mint! We don't have the time!
And computer code means we won't speak in rhyme!
I must speak to Ms. Claus to sort this all out,
And my throat is all sore from having to shout!"

Santa ran to his office and sat in his chair,
And complained to Ms. Claus as he pulled out his hair.
"The elves are on strike; the reindeer won't fly.
Why Mother, I don't even know why I try!"

"These kids don't ask
For things I can wrap.
All they ask for is gift cards or downloads or apps!"

"And that's just the start,
It only gets worse!
They're asking for bitcoin and tokens
For the Multiverse!"

"Oh Santa," she said.
"Now don't you despair,
The stockings will be hung
By the chimney with care."

Santa chewed on his beard and wrung his sore hands
While crying "Mother, you simply don't understand!
Most don't have chimneys, or even real trees!
And when they do
It's so hard on my knees!"

"My knees and my back
Are all out of whack,
From Two Thousand years
Of carrying that sack!"

"And for what, may I ask you?
Be they tall or quite small
The adults don't believe
I exist at all!"

"I mean Mother, just look at the news,
They don't want me to deliver to those without views.
Or to Buddhists, or Hindus or Muslims or Jews.
Wrapped up in religion,
They've all lost the point -
That CHILDREN are the reason
I started this joint!"

"I don't want them to focus
On a belief or creed,
Santa is about giving
To people in need."

"Or so Jesus taught me
When I was a boy.
When He sat down and showed me
How to make my first toy."

"But the elves don't think
I can run the workshop.
Perhaps I'm too old, perhaps I should stop.
I hardly think
That I will be missed.
Apparently, most adults
Don't think I exist."

"By popular opinion
It seems I've been fired.
Perhaps it is time
That Santa retired..."

Just then a young elf
Crept in to see
Why Santa was acting
So petulantly.
She climbed in his lap, and sat hand in hand,
And patiently tried
To make him understand.

"Your problem Santa, is just as you said.
You are trying to keep
Christmastime in your head.
Keep Christmastime in your heart
As you always have done,
And make it not about views;
But about kindness and fun."

"As long as the children care for all peoples,
They don't need a temple or cathedrals with steeples.
They just need to be generous and be of good cheer,
With charity for ALL at this time of the year."

And it dawned on Santa,
The young elf was right!
Change was inevitable,
There was no need to fight.
Because a heart that is heavy,
Works much better light.

Beliefs are important,
They help make our lives clear.
But you can celebrate all kinds
While you spread Christmas cheer.

And the gifts and the wrapping
Could come in new form,
If we ensure loving kindness
Persists as the norm.

And who cares if some adults
Don't think he exists.
The children believe,
And that's enough to persist!
Santa leapt to his feet and without a stop,
Ran as fast as he could, right back to his shop.

"Listen up all of you! I know what we'll do!
We'll address all these changes right AFTER we're through!
Your concerns are all noted, they have not diminished,
But they can all wait until Christmas is finished!"

The elves and the reindeer all gave a great cheer
Their changes could wait 'til the start of next year.
A Committee was formed without sides or allegiance,
And delegates appointed to address every grievance.

Santa leapt onto his sleigh,
And with a wave of his hat
Christmas was started.
And well, that was that.

So, Christmas went off
With no one to blame.

(except for ol' Prancer who filed his claim)

PICK UP MORE

AWARD-WINNING BOOKS BY BRIAN DONNELLY!

PRAISE FOR BRIAN DONNELLY'S CHILDREN'S BOOKS

5 / 5 Stars. "A great read for kids…" - Heidi Rojek, San Francisco Book Review

Clarion Rating: 4 out of 5 Stars. "Fun and humorous... The book's illustrations are adorable and detailed." - Forward Reviews

"This tale's jokes and triumphant ending will delight young readers."- Kirkus

"Illustrations are comical and add page turning energy." - The Children's Book Review

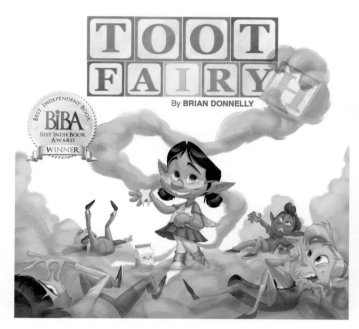

PRAISE FOR BRIAN DONNELLY'S CHILDREN'S BOOKS

"Fun, polished illustrations..the rhyming meter of the narrative is also entertaining and energetic." - Blue Ink Review

"Vivid and poly chromatic illustrations give depth to the story-line. Donnelly's rhyming prose lightens an otherwise heavy topic." - Book Life Review

ALL AVAILABLE ONLINE NOW ON AMAZON!

Made in the USA
Columbia, SC
14 December 2024

49302452R00018